The Adventure Continues . . .

Hi! I'm Jackie. I'm an archaeologist. I study ancient treasures to learn about the past.

My big adventure began when I found a golden shield in Bavaria, Germany, with an eight-sided stone in its center. It was a magical charm— a talisman!

Legend says that twelve talismans are scattered around the world. Each one has a picture of an animal on it. And each holds a different kind of magic.

All twelve talismans together have incredible power!

An evil group called The Dark Hand is looking for the talismans. They plan to use the awesome magic to rule the world!

That's why I have to find the talismans first.

It was easy to find the rooster talisman, but the ox talisman was hidden in a place you would never believe. . . .

A PARACHUTE PRESS BOOK

Published by Grosset & Dunlap, a division of Penguin Putnam Books for Young Readers, New York. GROSSET & DUNLAP is a trademark of Penguin Putnam, Inc. Published simultaneously in Canada. Printed in U.S.A.

Library of Congress Cataloging-in-Publication Data is available.

ISBN 0-448-42651-X
A B C D E F G H I J

JACKIE CHAN ADVENTURES™ #3

Sign of the Ox

A novelization by Megan Stine
based on the teleplay "The Mask of El Toro Fuerte"
written by Duane Capizzi

Grosset & Dunlap

"How can an old *Chinese* talisman be hidden in *Mexico*? It should be in China," Jackie Chan grumbled.

Jackie climbed the tall pyramid in Mexico. He climbed and climbed until he finally reached the top of the pyramid's steps, where an ancient temple stood.

Jackie stepped into the doorway of the temple. He knew it led to a secret chamber. Jackie started to enter, but then he stopped.

Did he hear a noise? Was someone following him?

No, it was probably just the wind, he decided.

But Jackie was very wrong. He *was* being followed—by five of his enemies! They all worked for The Dark Hand—a group of criminals who wanted to rule the world!

Their leader was named Valmont. Next to him stood a man named Finn. Finn watched Jackie through binoculars.

"Chan is almost inside," he said. "Let's go."

Inside the pyramid, Jackie shined his flashlight on the map he held in

2

his hand. It showed a picture of the treasure he was seeking—the ox talisman. The talisman was hidden inside a golden sculpture, carved in the shape of an ox head.

Jackie flashed the light over the temple walls.

"There it is." Jackie spotted the golden head. It hung in the center of a wall in the secret room.

He placed a finger inside each of the ox's nostrils. With a long, low creak, the ox jaw slowly opened.

Jackie gasped. The ox head contained a big, fat . . . nothing! The ox talisman was gone!

Valmont and his men burst into the room. "Where is it?" Valmont roared, staring into the empty ox head.

"I don't know," Jackie answered.

Valmont quickly tripped Jackie.

Jackie fell to the floor and Valmont pressed his knee into Jackie's chest. "Liar!" he shouted. "Maybe my friend Tohru can help you find the ox talisman!"

The floor shook as Tohru came into the secret room. He was taller and wider than ten grown men. His enormous body blocked out the light from the temple door.

Oh, no! Jackie thought. Not Tohru!

Tohru yanked Jackie off the ground, then held him upside down. "Where is the talisman?" Tohru boomed.

He shook Jackie to see if the talisman would fall out of his pocket.

Then he slammed Jackie against the wall and pinned him there with one huge hand.

"It's gone. Someone *else* must have found it," Jackie said.

"I do not believe you," Tohru said.

He pulled back his powerful arm and made a fist. He was ready to pound it into Jackie's head.

But before he could, a sound startled everyone.

"Mwoooowww!"

Jackie's eyes darted to a gigantic figure in the shadows.

Behind Tohru was a tall, scary mummy!

Chapter 2

The big mummy lurched forward. Its bony arms waved in the air. Its spooky wail filled the temple.

In an instant, Valmont and all his men rushed out of the secret room. All except for Tohru.

Jackie stared at the creepy mummy—and saw a girl walking behind it. It was Jade, he realized. His eleven-year-old niece! What was she doing there?

Jackie stared at the mummy even harder and saw that it wasn't real. It was a big puppet—and Jade was making it move! She held it in front of her with two long sticks.

"*Mwooooowww!*" Jade made the mummy wail.

Tohru gazed at the mummy in shock.

Here's my chance, Jackie thought. Swiftly, he pulled out of Tohru's grasp. He darted into the shadows of the chamber.

He leaped forward and whisked Jade under his arm, carrying her away like a football.

Then he dashed out of the pyramid chamber, down the steps, and into the jungle.

"Don't look back!" Jackie warned Jade. He still carried her as he ran.

But Jade couldn't help it. She could see the evil men at the bottom of the pyramid.

"Uh-oh, Jackie. Run faster!" she cried. "They're on motorbikes—and they're right behind us!"

Jackie ran harder. "Why are you here?" Jackie panted. "We made a deal. I let you come on this trip, but you were supposed to stay back at the hotel and do your homework!"

"Lucky for *you* I showed up!" Jade replied.

"Okay, that's true. Thank you," Jackie said. "But next time, don't finish your homework so quickly. It could be dangerous!"

Jade listened to the motorbikes roar through the jungle. They were closing in on them.

Then Jade saw where Jackie was headed. Straight for a hang glider. It was perched at the edge of a cliff.

A young man dressed in shorts and sandals stood next to it.

Jackie leaped for the hang glider, bumping the man aside.

"I'm-sorry-I'll-bring-it-right-back-thank-you!" Jackie cried out as he grabbed the glider with one hand. He held Jade with the other. The glider soared off the edge of the cliff, into the air.

"Wow!" Jade exclaimed.

She stared at the beautiful blue ocean below them.

Then she looked back at the cliff. Valmont and his men were stopped at the edge with their motorbikes. They could not follow.

This is what makes it so cool to be Jackie Chan's niece! she thought.

Jackie and Jade soared through the air. They flew over the hills of the pretty Mexican countryside.

"Let's land here," Jackie said.

He landed the hang glider, and soon Jackie and Jade walked into a small, busy town.

"Jade, I am going to ask if anyone here knows about the talisman." Jackie headed into a store. "Don't go anywhere."

"Uh, right," Jade said. Then, as soon as her uncle went into the store, she wandered toward some musicians.

"*Hola,*" a boy said to her. Jade knew that meant "hello" in Spanish.

She checked him out. The boy was about her age and height. He had dark, straight hair.

"I am Paco," the boy said. "What is a charming young woman such as yourself doing tonight?"

Jade's face went sour. "Ewww!" she cried. "Are you asking me on a *date?*"

Paco shook his head fast. "Oh, no, no, no!" he said quickly. "I am trying to get an audience for my hero—El Toro Fuerte!"

"El *who*-o *what*-ay?" Jade asked.

"El To-ro Fwair-tay!" Paco said slowly. He whipped out a small poster and handed it to her. On it was a picture of a wrestler wearing a mask. The words EL TORO FUERTE were at the top in large letters. In Spanish, that meant "The Strong Bull."

"El Toro is Mexico's mightiest wrestler!" Paco declared. "He has *never* lost a match. He will wrestle tonight."

Jade sneered. "Wrestling? Ha!" she said. "Everyone knows that wrestling is all fake."

"El Toro Fuerte is no fake," Paco insisted. "Nobody can beat him because he is the best!"

"Oh, yeah?" Jade said. "That's what *you* think. See that guy over there?" She pointed to Jackie. "*He* is the best wrestler in the world," Jade said.

"Him?" Paco laughed. "But he's just a little mouse-man."

"No way," Jade argued. "He can totally beat your guy."

"Can not," Paco said.

"Can, too," Jade said.

"Can not," Paco repeated.

"Can, too!" Jade said firmly.

"Humph," Paco folded his arms. "If you think so, then the two should meet. Don't you agree?"

"Definitely! You're on," Jade said with a nod.

"Good. Bring your mouse-man to the arena tonight," Paco said. "He will wrestle El Toro Fuerte. And then we will find out who is the best!"

Chapter 3

"No, Jade," Jackie told his niece a few minutes later. "I am not fighting anybody."

"But Jackie, you *have* to!" Jade said. "I told this boy that you were the best wrestler in the world. So now you have to prove it!"

Jackie bent down and put an arm around his niece. "Listen carefully, Jade. A person should not fight for the sake of fighting," he said. "Only fight when you have no other choice."

Jade nodded. "That's cool. And that's what will happen. When you get in the ring tonight, and this El Toro guy starts pounding you, you will have *no other choice*."

"That's not what I meant!" Jackie said.

"Please, Jackie," Jade begged him. "Besides, you have nothing better to do tonight."

"I don't?" Jackie said. "How about searching for the ox talisman?"

"But it could be anywhere on earth," Jade moaned. "It could be a million miles away."

True, Jackie thought.

He stared at the poster in Jade's hand. It was a picture of El Toro Fuerte, the wrestler.

And right there, sewn into the forehead of his mask, was the symbol of an ox!

Could that be the talisman? Jackie wondered.

"Okay," he told Jade. "We will go to the wrestling match tonight. Perhaps the talisman is right under my nose!"

The wrestling arena was filled with people yelling and cheering.

Paco was there waiting for Jade and Jackie. "I see you have brought the mouse-man to fight El Toro Fuerte," Paco said to Jade.

"No, no." Jackie sat down. "I did not come to fight." Jackie pulled out Jade's poster. He pointed to the ox symbol on El Toro Fuerte's mask.

"Paco, can you tell me what this is?" Jackie asked.

"It is the sign of El Toro Fuerte," Paco said. "El Toro is strong, just like an ox."

"I must speak to El Toro." Jackie jumped to his feet and headed backstage.

He had no trouble finding El Toro's dressing room.

Jackie knocked.

"Yes?" El Toro answered without opening the door.

"I'm from the laundry," Jackie said. "There's been a mix-up. Your

17

mask wasn't properly cleaned."

"No way!" El Toro cried. "El Toro Fuerte *never* removes his mask!"

Jackie's mind raced. There had to be some way to make El Toro open the door so that Jackie could see the mask.

Before Jackie could think of another trick, someone grabbed his ankles!

In an instant, Jackie was hanging upside down—in the grip of Tohru's huge, powerful hands!

Chapter 4

"Hello, Chan," Tohru rumbled.

Jackie swayed high above the ground. "Why do you keep doing this to me?" he asked.

Before Tohru could answer, Jackie moved with lightning speed. He swung his arms and grabbed the cuffs of Tohru's pants. Then he yanked hard!

The big bully's pants fell to the ground. Underneath, he was wearing boxer shorts. They had big smiley faces all over them.

"Huh?" Tohru grunted. He dropped Jackie to pull up his pants.

With a powerful kick of his legs, Jackie sent the big guy crashing to the floor.

Then he heard pounding foot-steps coming toward him. The other men of The Dark Hand were hot on his trail!

I'm out of here! Jackie thought. He dashed down the hall, searching for a place to hide.

Jackie tried the knobs on two dressing-room doors. Both were locked. He tried a third door and it opened.

Jackie slipped inside. The room

was empty. But hanging over a chair he found a blue-and-yellow mask and cape.

The perfect disguise!

Dressed in the costume, Jackie strolled into the hallway.

He took a deep breath, then walked right by the men from The Dark Hand.

Ha! They do not recognize me! Jackie smiled.

As he hurried toward the arena, he felt a firm hand on his shoulder.

"It's time," a man behind him said.

Time? Jackie wondered. Time for what?

The man shoved Jackie through a curtain—straight into the wrestling ring!

"Oh, no!" Jackie moaned. "My disguise fooled everyone. They think I am a wrestler!"

"Good evening, friends," the announcer said into a microphone. "Tonight, two giants will clash in this very ring!"

The crowd cheered.

Shouting above the crowd, he pointed to Jackie and said, "In this corner we have . . . The Masked Chicken."

Then he pointed to the champion. "And in this corner, El Toro Fuerte!"

The crowd went wild.

Wow, he's huge, Jackie thought, looking at the masked wrestler. Jackie stared at the ox talisman in the middle of the mask. The ox glowed!

"Tonight, one man will drink deep from the cup of victory," the announcer said. "And the other will be unmasked!"

Unmasked? That's very good! Jackie thought. If I can beat El Toro, I will grab the mask—and capture the ox talisman!

It looks like Jade is right this time, Jackie realized. I have no choice but to fight.

Jackie glanced into the stands. Jade and Paco sat right in front.

Ding! The bell rang to start the fight.

El Toro charged at Jackie, one massive shoulder aimed straight at Jackie's chest.

"*Oomph!*" Jackie flew into the

23

ropes. Then he bounced off the ropes onto the mat.

"Toro! Toro! Toro!" the crowd chanted.

Get up! Jackie told himself.

But his head was spinning. El Toro had amazing strength.

Slowly, Jackie staggered to his feet. "Okay," he said softly. "Time to get tough."

Jackie spun around to gain speed. Then he leaped forward and landed a perfect drop kick on El Toro's chest.

"Heeeeaiiii!" Jackie cried, letting all his energy flow into the move.

But El Toro reached out and snatched Jackie's feet. He stopped Jackie in midair!

The masked wrestler raised Jackie

high above his head, and threw him to the ground.

El Toro leaped into a dive. He landed on top of Jackie with a loud crushing thud.

"*Ohhhh,*" Jackie moaned. He tried to get up, but he couldn't move.

I must stand up, Jackie thought. I must!

He tried to lift his head, but he was too dizzy.

Jackie moaned again. "If I don't get up, I will lose the match—and the talisman!"

Chapter 5

The referee counted to three.

Jackie couldn't move.

"The winner!" the referee cried. "El Toro Fuerte!"

El Toro raised both arms high. The crowd screamed and cheered.

The referee leaned over Jackie and ripped off his mask.

The crowd cheered louder.

Jackie could hear the roar.

But he was dizzy. So dizzy.

A vision of his old uncle floated above him. Am I dreaming this? he wondered.

Then he heard Uncle's voice.

"Remember, Jackie," Uncle said. "Each talisman has a different magic."

"Yes, yes, Uncle," Jackie said to the vision. "Twelve animals. Like the Chinese zodiac."

"One more thing," Uncle said. "What happened to you? You lost the match so fast."

"I know," Jackie said, still lying on the mat. "He was so strong!"

"Hmm," Uncle said. "Maybe the power of the ox talisman is magical *strength*."

"Of course! Strength!" Jackie answered.

"One more thing," Uncle said.

With Uncle there is always one more thing, Jackie knew.

Uncle reached forward and bopped Jackie on the forehead.

"Ow!" Jackie moaned. Then he opened his eyes.

The vision of his uncle was gone. Jackie awoke to find Jade leaning over him.

"Jackie, get up!" she said. "The match is over. Everybody is gone."

"The ox talisman," Jackie said. "Uncle told me in a vision. It gives El Toro superhuman strength."

Jade stamped her foot. "I knew it!" she said angrily. "Wrestling is so *fake!*"

"Come on, Jade," Jackie said,

struggling to his feet. "I must find El Toro—before Valmont and his nasty thugs do."

But Jackie and Jade were too late.

Right outside the arena, they found Tohru and El Toro. Tohru towered over the wrestler.

"You must give me the mask," Tohru demanded. He lunged forward, trying to grab it.

El Toro was too fast for Tohru. In one smooth and powerful move, he hoisted Tohru over his head. He spun him around, and slammed him to the ground.

The force of the blow left an enormous hole in the street.

"Whoa!" Jade whispered. "He nailed Tohru! And *nobody* nails Tohru."

29

Paco stepped out from behind a parked car. "I told you El Toro was the best in the world," he bragged.

Paco beamed as El Toro strolled away.

"Yes," Jackie said. "With the power of the talisman, he is very strong. But he still isn't safe from Valmont. The Dark Hand will send more of its forces very soon."

"What are you going to do, Jackie?" Jade asked.

"I must warn El Toro right away," Jackie replied.

Jackie turned his head. He saw a flicker of movement in a dark alley.

"It is too late!" Jackie said. "They're here!"

Chapter 6

An army of shadowy figures fluttered through the alleys.

"They're here," Jackie repeated. "The Shadowkhan!" They were the ninjas sent by The Dark Hand to get the talisman.

"You two stay here," Jackie ordered. Then he bolted into the town square. He had to find El Toro.

But Jade and Paco didn't listen to Jackie. They raced toward the town square, too. They spotted Jackie and El Toro by a fountain.

Almost at once, the Shadowkhan were everywhere. They swooped through the square, blocking the exits.

"Look out, Jackie!" Jade called. She pulled Paco into a doorway, away from danger.

Swooosh! Three Shadowkhan swooped at Jackie, flipping him onto his back.

Jackie leaped up again, ready to fight. But two more Shadowkhan flew at him.

"Heeeaiiii!" Jackie cried, whirling and spinning to kick his attackers.

He grabbed a pole from a street sign and used it as a fighting stick.

"I *told* you Jackie rocks!" Jade said to Paco as they watched from the doorway.

"True," Paco admitted. "But El Toro is better."

"Is not," Jade argued.

"Is, too," Paco said.

"Is not," Jade said.

"Is, too," Paco repeated.

The army of ninjas was endless. More and more of the dark figures swarmed into the street.

One by one, they flew at El Toro. But each time, he tossed them aside.

"You see?" Paco said. "My hero is winning! He is the best!"

Jackie jumped in to help El Toro.

But El Toro didn't see who was coming at him. He grabbed Jackie

33

without looking and flung him aside.

Jackie hit a wall, then slid to the ground.

"Whoa! Your guy is *too* good!" Jade shook her head.

A moment later, one of the Shadowkhan flew to the top of a nearby building. He was swinging a long chain. On the end of the chain was a large suction cup.

The Shadowkhan swung the chain around and around and then—*Thwap!*

The suction cup landed on El Toro's head—and stuck to the mask.

The Shadowkhan yanked hard on the chain. With a loud sucking sound, the mask flew right off El Toro's head!

"What?" El Toro cried. A look of fear flashed on his unmasked face.

Two Shadowkhan whirled toward El Toro—and kicked him to the ground.

El Toro lay facedown in the dirt. Without the power of the ox talisman, his strength was gone.

"Noooo!" Paco cried when his hero was defeated.

"Jackie!" Jade called. Her eyes darted toward her uncle.

But Jackie still lay on the ground, knocked out by El Toro.

Jade watched Tohru march into the street. The Shadowkhan handed him the mask.

Tohru ripped the talisman from it. Then he headed for a Jeep that would take him back to The Dark Hand.

"Let's go," Tohru said to the driver.

But then he stopped and turned back.

What is he going to do now? Jade wondered. She trembled in the doorway.

Tohru stomped over to Jackie.

He stared down at Jackie's body, lying so still and helpless.

"Let's take him," Tohru said. "He'll be our prize!"

Jade watched in horror as he lifted Jackie with one hand, tossed him into the Jeep, and took off.

Chapter 7

"Jackie!" Jade cried.

She watched the Jeep disappear in a cloud of dust.

What was she going to do?

How was she going to save him?

Paco stood beside her, hanging his head. He stared at El Toro, still lying in the dirt.

"Jade was right," Paco said. "You *are* a fake!"

El Toro lifted his head and gazed

sadly at Paco. "I am sorry," he said.

"No time for sorry," Jade said.

Jade kneeled beside the wrestler. "Mr. Toro, you've got to get up. We've got to help Jackie!"

El Toro shook his head. "I can help no one," he replied. "Paco has spoken the truth—I am a fake."

"So what?" Jade said. "You can *try*, can't you? Come on, come on, come on! Get up!"

She tugged on him. But he was so heavy, she couldn't budge him.

"Without the power of the ox, I am nothing," El Toro moaned.

"No way!" Jade argued. "You've got to help Jackie!"

"What can I do without the mask?" El Toro said.

"Forget the mask!" Jade replied. "Jackie once told me, 'The wise seek power within themselves. The foolish seek it within others.'"

"Huh?" El Toro said.

Jade shrugged. "Yeah. I don't know where Jackie gets this stuff from. But you know what I *think* it means?"

"What?" El Toro asked.

"It means, *you are not going to let a little girl go fight those bad boys all by herself, are you?*"

"I guess not," the wrestler said. He dragged himself to his feet.

"We'll be back soon, Paco!" Jade called. Together she and El Toro raced to find Jackie.

Their trail led to a private airport in the middle of the jungle. Tohru and Finn were getting ready to take off in a small plane.

"Look—in the plane!" Jade cried. "Finn is tying Jackie up!"

Jade could see that Jackie's arms were completely tied to his body with rope. But his legs were still free.

Jade thought fast.

She hopped onto El Toro's shoulders so she could reach the door of the plane.

"Knock, knock," Jade said, staring into the open hatchway.

Finn dropped the rope he was using to tie Jackie. He glared at Jade. "Why, you little meddler," he said. "I'll teach you some manners."

Jackie flew into action. He planted a karate kick on Finn. It sent the man sailing across the cargo space and out of the plane. Finn landed on the ground with a thud, knocked out cold.

"Hurray! My plan worked!" Jade cheered.

El Toro reached into the plane and pulled Jackie out. He set him on the ground.

"*Hola*, Jackie!" Jade said, smiling. "That's Spanish for 'hello!'"

The plane's engines started.

"No! No! Don't let them take off!" Jackie cried. "The talisman is on board!"

Jackie's arms and hands were still tied to his body.

Jade knew that it was up to her to save the talisman.

In a flash, she leaped onto El Toro's shoulders again. Then she hopped into the plane.

El Toro followed her.

Jackie watched in horror as the hatchway closed—and the plane began to move.

He was still tied up.

And the other end of the rope was coiled around a big metal wheel—inside the plane!

Slowly, the plane started down the runway. Then faster. And faster.

"Whaaaa?" Jackie cried as he ran to keep up with the moving plane.

He ran as fast as he could.

But the plane slowly lifted off the ground.

And Jackie's feet lifted into the air.

"Pull me in!" he cried.

Jade ran to the hatchway and opened it. She grabbed the rope. She tugged on it with all her might, trying to pull Jackie into the plane.

"I'm not strong enough!" she cried.

Wait a second, Jade thought. Not *strong* enough? I would be—if I had the ox talisman!

She raced to the cockpit to get the ox talisman. It sat in a wooden box on the empty seat next to the pilot.

She grabbed it.

"Oh, no, you don't!" the pilot said. He reached for the box.

"Oh, no, *you* don't!" Jade shot back. "Heeeyah!"

She leaped and kicked—and

43

knocked the pilot out cold.

"Yes!" Jade cheered, shooting a fist into the air. "Look at me—I'm Jackie Chan!"

Then she felt the plane begin to dive.

"Uh-oh," she moaned.

She stared at the pilot she had knocked out.

No one was flying the plane.

They were going to crash!

Chapter 8

Meanwhile, Jackie was in even bigger trouble. The rope he was tied with was unraveling. At any second, it would snap and drop him to the ground below!

Ping! The rope snapped in two. Jackie started to fall.

But at the last second, he twisted around and grabbed the end of the rope. Using all his strength, he slowly began to climb up the rope.

He reached the opening of the plane and dragged himself inside. Yes!

In the big open cargo space, El Toro and Tohru were fighting.

Jackie looked into the cockpit. He saw the pilot lying on the floor.

"Hey!" Jackie yelled at them. "Who is flying the plane?"

El Toro and Tohru suddenly stopped fighting.

"Aaahhhhh!" they all cried at once. The plane was diving straight down!

They scrambled into the cockpit.

They found Jade pulling on the controls as hard as she could. Slowly, the plane began to lift again.

"Hey! I could use a little help here," Jade said.

"Oh, right!" Jackie reached over Jade's shoulders to help.

Together, the two of them brought the plane down for a safe landing.

The plane rolled to a stop in the middle of a small town.

Paco was waiting there for them there. Somehow, he had found them.

Jade, Jackie, El Toro, and Tohru climbed out of the plane. The three men faced one another again, ready to fight.

"El Toro Fuerte, you are no longer my hero!" Paco cried.

"Not so fast, Paco," Jade whispered to herself. She scrambled back into the plane and grabbed the box with the ox talisman.

"Mr. Toro!" Jade called to the wrestler. "Catch!"

She threw the ox talisman to him, and he caught it.

El Toro looked at the talisman for a moment, then shook his head. "No, thank you, Jade," he said. "I would rather lose with dignity than win by cheating."

He tossed the ox talisman back to her.

"Ohhh-kaaay," Jade said, not sounding so sure.

Everyone whirled into action. Jackie and El Toro battled Tohru bravely. But the huge man was one hundred times stronger than even the two together.

Tohru easily lifted Jackie with one

48

hand and El Toro with the other. He threw them both through a brick wall.

Jackie and El Toro lay on the ground in a heap of brick rubble.

Tohru hovered above them, his body as big as a building. "*Now* tell me who is the mightiest one?" he demanded.

But before Jackie could answer, Jade leaped into Tohru's path. "I'll give you a hint!" she answered.

Jackie saw something flash on Jade's belt.

He stared at it. It flashed again, and then it began to glow.

Jade was wearing the ox talisman!

Jade flew at Tohru.

"Heeeeyahhh!" she cried, leaping

like a tiger. She struck his chest with an awesome force.

The huge man sailed across the town square. He hit a brick building so hard, the whole building toppled down on him.

Jade dusted off her hands and grinned. She rubbed the talisman. "Can I keep it?" she asked Jackie.

"No!" Jackie said firmly.

"Awww," Jade complained. "You spoil all my fun!"

"El Toro Fuerte?" Paco gazed up at his hero.

The wrestler hung his head in shame—embarrassed that Tohru had defeated him.

"Will you teach me the ways of the wrestler?" Paco asked.

"Really?" El Toro Fuerte looked surprised. "Why, yes. With all the wisdom of my experience."

"You are the greatest," Paco declared happily.

Jade stomped her foot. "No way. *Jackie's* the greatest."

"No. El Toro," Paco said.

"Jackie!" Jade said.

"El Toro!" Paco argued.

"Jackie!" Jade shot back.

Jackie watched his niece with a smile. He didn't care who was the better fighter.

He was just glad that they had found the ox talisman—and kept it from The Dark Hand.

A letter to you from Jackie

Dear Friends,

In the _Sign of the Ox_ Jade wants me to fight El Toro Fuerte. She wants me to show everyone how brave I am. But I tell her: Never fight for the sake of fighting.

I learned when I was very young not to fight. Bravery does not mean power on the outside. It means wisdom on the inside.

Believe it or not, I used to be a fighter. My classmates and I would get into arguments over silly stuff all the time. At first I wanted to prove my point by using force.

Then we started training in martial arts with our master. He taught us many valuable things. We practiced self-defense exercises over and over. We were never taught to be the attacker. We were taught to think and _react_ to a situation.

Our master always said that fighting for no reason is the way of the coward. It took some time to understand, but I now know that he was right. Of course, he was the master!

Pretty soon I realized that every time I fought

on the playground, somebody got hurt. And some-
times that somebody was me! Either way, it never
felt good when it was all over. Nobody ever seems
to learn anything from a fight.

Even now, when you see me battling with the
guys from The Dark Hand, I'll never start a fight.
That's because I still remember the lessons I was
taught.

Fighting is for cowards. And I'm not a coward. I
bet you're not either.

Here's another little secret for you. When you
watch JACKIE CHAN ADVENTURES and my
movies, you'll notice something that makes my
action scenes different. When I get hit, I say, "Ow!"

I am not a superhero. I am a real human being,
just like you. Fighting hurts, and I want everybody
to remember that.

Find out what happens in the next book

#4 Enter...the Viper

The snake talisman is in New York City. Jackie's in a race against the evil Dark Hand to find it. Who will get there first?

Enter the

JACKIE CHAN ADVENTURES™

Ultimate Fan Sweepstakes!
— NO PURCHASE NECESSARY —

Are you the Ultimate Fan?
Enter today and you could be a lucky winner of one of the following great *Jackie Chan Adventures* prizes:

1 Grand Prize
Win a *Jackie Chan Adventures* Ultimate Fan Gift Pack!
Includes the first five Jackie Chan Adventures books autographed by Jackie Chan, T-shirt, video, action figures, sticker activity pack, board game, backpack, video game, and other cool *Jackie Chan Adventures* gifts!

5 First Prizes
Win the first five *Jackie Chan Adventures* books, including an autographed copy of #1 THE DARK HAND!

50 Second Prizes
Win a copy of *Jackie Chan Adventures* #5 SHENDU ESCAPES!

Complete this entry form or hand print all of the information listed below on a 3' x 5' card (see Official Rule #2) and send it to:

Jackie Chan Adventures Ultimate Fan Sweepstakes
Village Station
P. O. Box 1045
New York, NY 10014

Name _____

Address _____

City _____

State _____ **Zip** _____

Phone _____ **Birthdate** __/__/__

Jackie Chan Adventures™ Ultimate Fan Sweepstakes Official Rules

1. **NO PURCHASE NECESSARY**. A purchase will not improve your chances of winning.

2. To enter complete the official entry form or hand print your name, address, age, and phone number along with the words "JACKIE CHAN ADVENTURES Ultimate Fan Sweepstakes" on a 3" x 5" card and mail to: JACKIE CHAN ADVENTURES Ultimate Fan Sweepstakes, Village Station, P. O. Box 1045, New York, NY 10014, postmarked **no later than January 31, 2002**. Enter as often as you wish, but each entry must be mailed separately. One entry per envelope. Partially completed, illegible, or mechanically reproduced entries will not be accepted. Sponsor is not responsible for lost, late, mutilated, illegible, stolen, postage due, incomplete, or misdirected entries. All entries become the property of Penguin Putnam Inc., and will not be returned.

3. The sweepstakes is open to legal residents of the United States and Canada (excluding Quebec), between the ages of five and twelve as of January 31, 2002, except as set forth below. Void in Puerto Rico and wherever prohibited or restricted by law. All federal, state, and local laws apply. In the event a winner is a Canadian resident, he or she must answer a time-limited skill question consisting of an arithmetical problem to be determined a winner. Sony Pictures Entertainment Inc., Kids' WB!, Adelaide Productions, Inc., Penguin Putnam Inc., Parachute Properties and Parachute Press, Inc. (individually and collectively "Parachute"), their respective officers, directors, shareholders, employees, suppliers, parents, subsidiaries, affiliates, agencies, sponsors, participating retailers, and persons connected with the use, marketing or conduct of this sweepstakes are not eligible. And family members living in the same household as any of the individuals referred to in the immediately forgoing sentence are not eligible.

4. Odds of winning depend on the total number of entries received. All prizes will be awarded. Winners will be randomly drawn on or about February 15, 2002, by Penguin Putnam Inc., whose decisions are final. Potential winners will be notified by mail and will be required to sign and return an affidavit of eligibility, release of liability, and all other legal documents which the sweepstakes sponsor may require (including a W-9 tax form) within 14 days of notification or an alternate winner will be selected. Prizes won by minors will be awarded to their parent or legal guardian who must sign and return all required legal documents. By acceptance of their prize, winners or winners' parents on winners' behalf consent to the use of their names, photographs, likeness, and personal information by Penguin Putnam, Parachute, Sony Pictures Entertainment, Adelaide, or Kids' WB!, and for any advertising, promotion, or publicity purposes without further compensation except where prohibited.

5. a) One (1) **Grand Prize Winner** wins a JACKIE CHAN ADVENTURES Ultimate Fan Gift Pack which includes the first five JACKIE CHAN ADVENTURES books autographed by Jackie Chan, T-shirt, video, action figures, board game, sticker activity pack, backpack, video game and other Jackie Chan Adventures product. Approximate retail value $100.00.

b) Five (5) **First Prize Winners** win the first five JACKIE CHAN ADVENTURES books, including an autographed copy of Book #1 THE DARK HAND. Approximate retail value $24.95.

c) Fifty (50) **Second Prize Winners** win a copy of JACKIE CHAN ADVENTURES Book #5 SHENDU ESCAPES. Approximate retail value $4.99.

6. Only one prize will be awarded per individual, family, or household. Prizes are non-transferable and cannot be sold or redeemed for cash. No cash substitute is available. Any federal, state, or local taxes are the responsibility of the winner. Sponsor may substitute prize of equal or greater value, if necessary, due to availability.

7. Additional terms: By participating, entrants agree a) to the official rules and decisions of the judges, which will be final in all respects; and to waive any claim to ambiguity of the official rules and b) to release, discharge, and hold harmless Penguin Putnam, Parachute, Sony Pictures Entertainment, Kids' WB!, Adelaide and their respective officers, directors, shareholders, employees, suppliers, parents, subsidiaries, affiliates, agencies, sponsors, participating retailers and persons connected with the use, marketing or conduct of this sweepstakes from and against any and all liability or damages associated with acceptance, use, or misuse of any prize received in this sweepstakes.

8. Any dispute arising from this sweepstakes will be determined according to the laws of the State of New York, without reference to its conflict of law principles, and the entrants consent to the personal jurisdiction of the State and Federal courts located in New York County and agree that such courts have exclusive jurisdiction over all such disputes.

9. To obtain the name of the winners, please send your request and a self-addressed stamped envelope to JACKIE CHAN ADVENTURES Ultimate Fan Sweepstakes, Village Station, P. O. Box 1045, New York, NY 10014 by March 1, 2002. Sweepstakes Sponsor: Penguin Putnam Inc.